September 21, 1981

The Gigantic Balloon

RUTH PARK

Illustrated by
KILMENY & DEBORAH NILAND

Parents' Magazine Press

NEW YORK

THE
GIGANTIC
BALLOON

Once upon a time, in Sydney, Australia,
there lived two shopkeepers. The tall one with the short hat
was Mr. J. J. Jones, owner of J. J. Jones's Gigantic Emporium.
The short one with the tall hat was Mr. Alexander Hoy,
proprietor of Hoy's Palace of Fashion and Universal Providers.
Each man was determined to sell more than his rival could.

Mr. Hoy was winning the contest, because he
and his sly helper, Titus Duckmallow,
thought up the cleverest advertising schemes.

Their advertisements were so popular that they
made Mr. Jones rant and rave. He was especially nasty
to his young assistant, Peter Thin.

Peter Thin did all the dirty jobs
other people in
J. J. Jones's Gigantic Emporium
didn't want to do.

He was often bullied and scolded, but Peter
kept his heart light because he had a secret dream.
"Someday," he told his dog Belle, "you and I
are going to share a great adventure. I don't know
how or when, but we shall."

Peter admired the latest advertisement for a monster sale
at Hoy's Palace of Fashion and Universal Providers,
which had floated down from a box kite high in the sky.
"Wouldn't it be grand to fly as free as the wind?"
he said to Belle.

The box kites made Mr. Jones turn red with rage and envy.
"I'll outsmart that fat rascal yet!" he shouted.
"Wait till he sees this." And he called Peter.
"Here, boy, go and paste up these handbills!"

Peter Thin read one handbill first.

"Oh, Belle!" he said excitedly.

"Mr. Jones has ordered a gigantic balloon from France —
and a fearless French balloonist to fly it!
It will trail a banner a hundred feet long, saying
'SHOP ONLY AT JONES'S, CHEAPEST AND CHOICEST.'
If only I were that fearless balloonist!"

Within a few weeks a huge packing case
arrived at J. J. Jones's.
In it was the gigantic balloon.
But the fearless balloonist remained home in France,
because Mr. Hoy had sent him a letter saying
that smallpox, measles and yellow-spotted fever
were very bad in Sydney.
Mr. Jones was heartbroken.
"A balloon with no balloonist!" he moaned.
"Everyone will laugh at me,
  especially Alexander Hoy!"

Up stepped Peter Thin. "I shall be your balloonist," he said.
He waited for Mr. Jones to bellow with rage, but he didn't.
Peter explained his dream.
"In my heart," he said, "I am not Peter Thin, shop assistant,
but a great adventurer. I shall become the celebrated
Pierre Maigre, fearless balloonist."

"What have I got to lose?" sighed Mr. Jones.

All night long the staff of J. J. Jones's Gigantic
Emporium worked to transform Peter into Pierre.
Belle wanted to watch but she was chased outside.
There she saw Mr. Hoy and the sly Titus Duckmallow
prowling around, trying to discover
what was happening.
"They're up to something!" whispered Mr. Hoy.
Titus Duckmallow gave Belle a swift kick.
"I'll get you for that," she growled.

Next day, the whole town went wild.
"Balloon!…J. J. Jones's!…Pierre Maigre!" was heard
on every side. Cheering crowds set off for the city park
where the balloon was being filled with gas.

Belle wanted to run beside Peter, but she couldn't get near him.
She was soon lost among the legs of the crowd.
One pair of those legs belonged to sly Titus Duckmallow,
but Belle never got close enough to bite him.

The Lord Mayor made a speech
praising Mr. Jones
and the fearless balloonist.
Mr. Hoy raised his tall hat to
Mr. Jones and tried to look sad.
Everyone cheered.

Belle, meanwhile, was following
a pair of long striped legs,
hoping for a good nip.
That's how she came to see
Titus Duckmallow
secretly fasten the basket
of the balloon
to two pegs he drove
into the ground.
She howled for Peter
to come and see.
"Stop that racket!"
said a man nearby
and he tied Belle
to the mayor's sun umbrella.

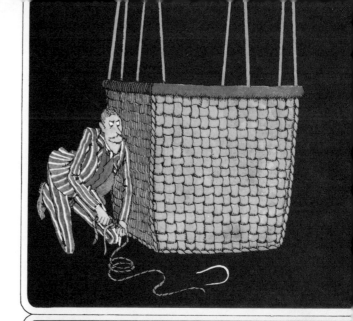

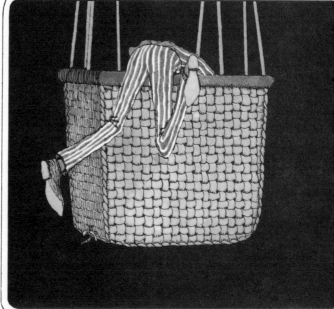

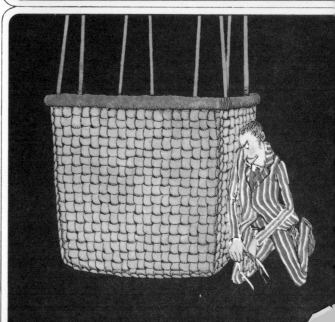

Peter Thin climbed into the basket.
It was full of packets of raisins,
chocolates, dog biscuits and other choice tidbits
for Peter to shower upon the delighted crowd
once the balloon had ascended.
Mr. Hoy took out a big handkerchief
and pretended to cry.
Peter threw out the sandbags
which weighted down the balloon.
Mr. Jones grandly cut the anchor rope
and announced,
"The gigantic balloon will now ascend!"

But it didn't. It just bumped a bit on the ground.
The crowd thought it had been tricked
and went crazy with disappointment.
"Catch that fake balloonist!" people screeched.
"Duck him in the fountain!"

There was almost a riot. Hoy was delighted.
Peter felt terrible.
"Help!" he cried. "Help me, Belle."
And Belle did.

She tugged at the pegs
and Peter saw the hidden rope.

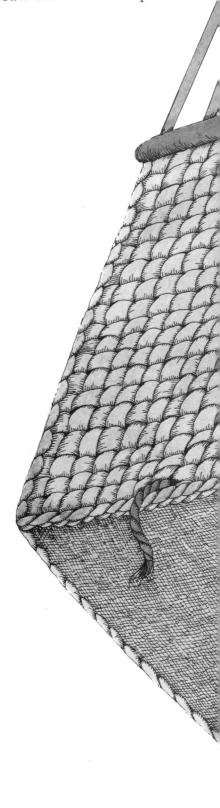

The gigantic balloon rose over the city.
What a wondrous sight!
As it floated past the tallest spire of
Hoy's Palace of Fashion and Universal Providers,
Peter unfurled the great banner
that could be seen for miles —
SHOP ONLY AT JONES'S,
CHEAPEST AND CHOICEST.

Mr. Hoy kicked Titus Duckmallow into the fountain.
But Mr. Jones shouted in triumph, "What loyalty!
Come back, Peter Thin, come back,
and I'll promote you to manager!"

But he was too late. Peter Thin, shop assistant,
was no more. In the gigantic balloon stood
the fearless balloonist Pierre Maigre.
He and his faithful friend Belle were off at last,
soaring free as the wind,
on their great adventure.